Awakened Skeleton

A Roleplaying Game Supplement

By Anthony Uyl

Ingersoll, Ontario, Canada 2020

Awakened Skeleton

A Roleplaying Game Supplement

Written by Anthony Uyl

Artwork by Christopher Cortright

Cover and interior background designs done by Lord Zsezse Works

See page 26 and 27 for Product Identity and Open Gaming Content information.

What kind of stories do you have?
Let us know!

Contact us at: solacegames@hotmail.com

See the full catalogue of Devoted Publishing and Solace Games books at:
http://www.lulu.com/spotlight/devotedpublishing

Published in Ingersoll, Ontario, Canada 2020

ISBN: 978-1-77356-411-1

Table of Contents

Introduction

When writing a game book, you always need to consider one important thing: What would be *fun* to play? Anyone that knows me knows I love playing dead things or playing characters that control dead things. I do not know why I enjoy doing this, but it is something all my friends have come to expect. Most wizard player characters wait and wait for a time to cast *fireball*, I wait to cast *animate dead.*

I wanted this option of the Awakened Skeleton to be as complete as possible. I am sure there are other things that some gamemasters and their players would like to see in a supplement of this type, but there has to be a point at which you stop and say that what you have written should be enough to get anyone started.

You see, half the fun of any roleplaying game is the ability to create, to dream about some fantasy adventure and the crazy things you can do to make your imaginings happen. It does not have to be rooted in reality, just reach out and think to yourself, "will this be fun?" If the answer is, "yes!" then find a way to make it happen!

I have given as many options for players to use to create a new and unique Awakened Skeleton each time they play one. Not only that, but the class options that come with this work should give any character some options to delve into the darker side of magical and fantasy realities.

Lastly, on the very first page of Chapter I you will notice the new skeleton race will have an ancient Koine (Common) Greek name with it. This is simply a more arcane way for you to refer to the race. Of course, you can completely disregard this and move on with the rest of the work, but I find using strange and ancient languages a joy for creating mystery around old ideas.

Have fun!

Anthony Uyl
- Author and Publisher

Chapter I - Race: Awakened Skeleton

Awakened Skeleton

Ηξυπνιζσε Οστεον ***(ēxypnixse osteon, Awakened Bone)***

Awoken by ancient magic or the curse of some angered god, the awakened are now living once more, sort of. Although Awakened Skeletons are not technically alive, they have all the memories and feelings that they once had when they were. While most of these memories and emotions can be somewhat disorienting and cause them some confusion, the awakened have a mission in this unlife that they feel only they can fulfill.

Many people are scared off by Awakened Skeletons. Most times, the first instance that they enter a community the guards and townspeople will either attack the awakened or runaway with a misunderstanding of who or what they are. The people have a right to be scared. The awakened know this. Many that have risen in the same way, brought great grief to the towns in the region they originally died.

Trying to maintain a normal life, just doing basic things, is difficult. Even if the community the awakened calls home has accepted them, there are some that are still wary. They are different, bred of evil, this makes a fair number of citizens afraid to even interact with them in any way.

Physical Description

Most Awakened Skeletons look similar. There is not much that will set them apart. The only things that make them different is if they are originally of a race unlike humans. For instance: dwarves, halflings, gnomes and orcs, whose skeletal anatomy all look different from what people are accustomed to. Sometimes even these differences will help feed the fear that people show towards them.

Unless they are of a different race than human, the different look they have, a gangly skeleton, is unnerving. There are people that see past the undead physical look to see that these awakened really heroes of sorts. But this appearance is enough to scare most people away. As charming as they were in life, the fear that people feel towards an awakened's physical appearance will never totally disappear.

Society

There has never been a true gathering of Awakened Skeletons that could be called a proper society. Most of these creatures are solo wanderers that go from town to town looking for work or victims. Anytime a society of them have formed, it has been under the tyrannical rule of a necromancer, liche or vampire.

A lot of Awakened Skeletons also fear the greater culture in forming a place of their own. The fear that would be generated would probably be responsible for military action against them. Since there are typically so few of the awakened to form a proper military, they would not stand a chance against a campaign by some paladin, a cleric or druid to purge the land of the filth of these undead. A more progressive society may allow for a town of skeletons to exist, but so far none have been forward thinking enough to allow for such a thing to happen. Maybe one day, the Awakened Skeletons can gather and create their own culture, but as of right now, they will have to suffer with the fear that causes them to have to sneak around to avoid being destroyed.

Relations

Most times, Awakened Skeletons will have difficulty building relations with anyone that is still alive. This can cause great distress to those that are trying to atone for some wrong, but fear is a powerful emotion that will force most people to keep them away. This sometimes will cause the awakened to seek interaction with other undead, mostly sentient ones, like themselves. While not all undead are welcoming of Awakened Skeletons, some are but will demand servitude of them to get acceptance. Those awakened that are trying to build a new, better life for themselves will often have to turn this offer down as it will cause them to do great evil that they were trying to atone for. Other more, degenerate awakened, will have no problem accepting these terms as revenge is something that might suit them.

Alignment and Religion

Not all Awakened Skeletons devote themselves to a god. Some are bitter that they have been raised to unlife, while others are thankful. Those that are angry about their new state, often find it difficult to make their way in the world. The awakened are after all, magical creatures, and since most magics emanate from a god of some sort, to totally reject the gods is almost unheard of for them.

Those that do become god fearing undead usually have two options for the type of gods they will follow. The obvious is gods like Orcus, or some other fantasy god of death. Those that follow the classical pantheons may have the awakened follow a god like Hades (Greek), Nephthys (Egyptian) or Hel (Norse). Of course, each awakened can feel free to follow whichever god of their choosing. The choice is ultimately theirs.

There are the aberrant Awakened Skeletons however that choose to follow a good god of light and life. Those that do this are usually seeking for redemption or even to be made truly alive again. Although most of the awakened realize this is more of a fantasy than an actual realization, they do hope for redemption of some kind in the underworld, if they make it back there again.

Adventurers

Those Awakened Skeletons that do not find a place in a community to call home, will often take on an adventuring life. These questing dead are mostly hoping to either cause as much mayhem as possible or are trying to find a hope

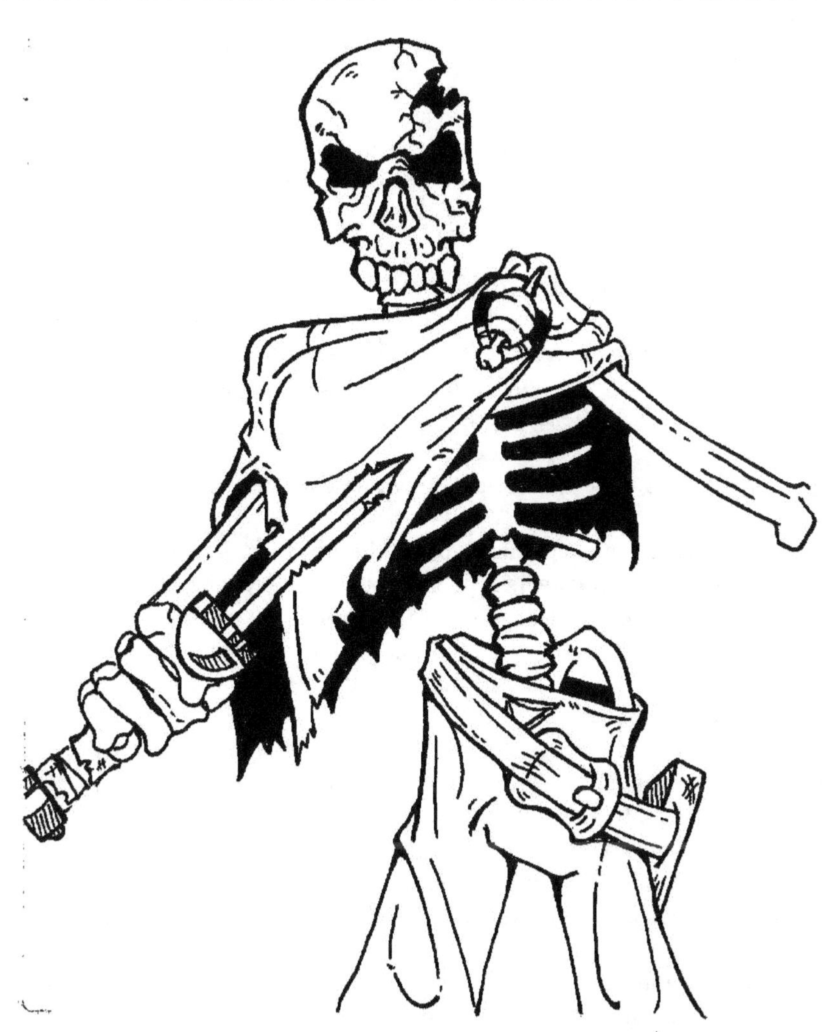

An Awakened Skeleton

that there is a meaning to this unlife, possibly even redemption. Most realize that they will never find a true place within society. Mostly the awakened hope that they will find an accepting group of travellers that will take on the service of the undead. Of course, these groups will also consider how they will be looked at, as morally upright people, having a skeleton with them!

Skeleton Names

Most Awakened Skeletons will decide to keep the names they had in life. Others will assume their own as a part of a new identity for their new life. These new names usually have some link to an evil personage or deity, but not always. Some try to pick a name that speaks of redemption as the newly Awakened Skeleton tries to right the wrong done to them, or that they did to someone else while they were alive.

Awakened Skeleton Racial Traits

Your Awakened Skeleton character has the following traits:

Ability Score Increase. You have no biological parts that would cause you to feel pain and be slowed down. You can be heavily damaged and still not have it phase you. Your Dexterity score increases by +2 and your Constitution score increases by +1.

No Anatomy. You are immune to poison damage and the poisoned condition.

Bone. When you are reduced to zero hit points, make a Constitution save DC 10 + whatever additional hit points would have brought you below zero. If you succeed, you are instead reduced to 1 hit point, but may take no actions except to heal yourself. Once you receive at least 5 additional hit points (bringing you to a minimum of 6), you can once again take regular actions in each of your turns.

You can only do this once per day and the use refreshes after a long rest.

Darkvision. Your vision is magical. You can see in dim light within 60 feet of you as if it were bright light, and in darkness as if it were dim light. You cannot discern colour in darkness, only shades of gray.

Healed by Necrotic Energy. You are healed by necrotic energy. Whenever you take damage from a necrotic attack, the damage inflicted instead heals you by that amount.

Undeath. Raised as a being of undeath, you count as an undead creature for all spells and abilities that affect undead. You are immune to disease and treat exhaustion as if it were one level less. You do not need to eat, drink, breathe or sleep, and you cannot ingest food or drink. Instead of sleeping, you enter an inactive state for 4 hours each day. You do not dream in this state; you are fully aware of your surroundings and notice approaching enemies and other events as normal.

Immortal. You do not age. Given time, the necromantic energies that sustain you will heal most wounds you take at approximately the same rate as a mortal, and your hit dice function as normal.

Fear. Your visage as a fleshless skeleton is unsettling to most people. You gain proficiency with the Intimidation skill.

Languages. You can speak, read, and write Common and one language available to the race you chose for your past life.

Awakened Skeleton Sub-Races

The options below are for those that want to add more detail and background to their Awakened Skeleton character. These sub-races are simply the classic races found in the core rulebook that allow you to pick a specific race of origin for your undead character.

Realize that even though your character may come from one of these races, the chances are that they will not accept you in your undead state. Of course, this all largely depends on the groups alignment that you are trying to affiliate with. Not all evil groups will however allow an undead creature to lurk inside their camp or community.

Dragonborn

These awakened are usually as honourable in unlife as they were in life. But this is not always the case. Some see their new lot in life and decide to go in the opposite direction and become dishonourable and chaotic. It is an unwritten part of dragonborn honour to destroy these creatures on sight, but they have proven to be a difficult group of undead to get rid of. As strong as their parent race, these awakened have proven to be formidable warriors.

Ability Score Increase. Your Strength score increases by +1.

Table: Draconic Ancestry

Dragon	*Damage Type*	*Breath Weapon*
Black	Acid	5 by 30 ft. line (Dex. save)
Blue	Lightning	5 by 30 ft. line (Dex. save)
Brass	Fire	5 by 30 ft. line (Dex. save)
Bronze	Lightning	5 by 30 ft. line (Dex. save)
Copper	Acid	5 by 30 ft. line (Dex. save)
Gold	Fire	15 ft. cone (Dex. save)
Green	Poison	15 ft. cone (Con. save)
Red	Fire	15 ft. cone (Dex. save)
Silver	Cold	15 ft. cone (Con. save)
White	Cold	15 ft. cone (Con. save)

Draconic Ancestry. You have draconic ancestry. Choose one type of dragon from the Draconic Ancestry table. Your breath weapon and damage resistance are determined by the dragon type, as shown in the table.

Breath Weapon. You can use your action to exhale destructive energy. Your draconic ancestry determines the size, shape, and damage type of the exhalation.

When you use your breath weapon, each creature within the exhalation must make a saving throw, the type of which is determined by your draconic ancestry. The DC for this saving throw equals 8 + your Constitution modifier + your proficiency bonus. A creature takes 2d6 damage on a failed save, and half as much damage on a successful one. The damage increases to 3d6 at 6th level, 4d6 at 11th level, and 5d6 at 16th level.

After you use your breath weapon, you cannot use it again until you complete a short or long rest.

Damage Resistance. You have resistance to the damage type associated with your draconic ancestry.

Dwarf

While most people are not accustomed to seeing an undead dwarf, they do exist. The dwarven community at large tries to deny the existence of awakened dead dwarves. Those that do accept that they are in fact roaming the countryside will often declare holy quests to rid the land of them. These awakened undead dwarves will run in fear of these holy crusaders as they are a fearsome lot to fight off.

Ability Score Increase. Your Constitution score increases by an additional +1.

Combat Training. You have proficiency with the battleaxe, handaxe, light hammer, and warhammer.

Tool Proficiency. You gain proficiency with the artisan's tools of your choice: smith's tools, brewer's supplies, or mason's tools.

Elf

These Awakened Undead are an abomination to all elves. Even the Drow who are inherently evil, view these creatures as things to be destroyed. There are those among the dark elves that would like to enslave them, but for the most part Drow hunt these creatures down. While the awakened undead elf may not appear as they once did, the awakened still has the intellectual and charismatic grace that so often accompanies those of its kin that are still alive.

Ability Score Increase. Your Intelligence score increases by +1.

Keen Senses. You have proficiency in the Perception skill.

Fey Ancestry. You have advantage on saving throws against being charmed, and magic cannot put you to sleep.

Gnome

Usually found among the trees and wilds of the region, these Awakened Skeletons suffer from a wide range of abuse from those they interact with. While often not realizing their new demeanor, many try to go into communities and deal with people just as they did when they were alive. They continue to tinker with toys and other mechanics, trying to improve them. Many living people see these new devices as cursed that may possibly spread the curse of unlife to them.

Ability Score Increase. Your Intelligence score increases by +1.

Size. Awakened Skeleton Gnomes are between 3 and 4 feet tall and average about 40 pounds. Your size is Small.

Speed. Your base walking speed is 25 feet.

Gnome Cunning. You have advantage on all Intelligence, Wisdom, and Charisma saving throws against magic.

A Dragonborn Awakened Skeleton

Half-Elf

Indistinguishable from elf and human Awakened Skeletons, these undead will face a lot of the same problems that others of their mixed heritage do. Many try to ply their skills in a profitable way, as the half-elf awakened tend to have a special skill set that some others do not. Still, they are mostly forced out of villages and towns, made to wander the wilderness, hoping that some vigilant crusader will not cut them down during their travels.

Ability Score Increase. You gain +1 to any one ability score of your choice, except Dexterity.

Fey Ancestry. You have advantage on saving throws against being charmed, and magic cannot put you to sleep.

Skill Versatility. You gain proficiency in one skill of your choice.

Half-Orc

Some of the most fearsome of the Awakened Skeletons that walk the wilderness. Most of these awakened have given in to their orc parentage, fighting and killing their fill everywhere they go. They give in to the rage almost more than a living orc. They just do not care. All these feelings of anger and the desire for blood make them unable to discern right from wrong. Some have fought their inner orc nature, but this is a path only the strongest can walk.

Ability Score Increase. Your Strength score increases by +1.

Menacing. You gain proficiency in the Intimidation skill.

Savage Attacks. When you score a critical hit with a melee weapon attack, you can roll one of the weapon's damage dice one additional time and add it to the extra damage of the critical hit.

Halfling

Being as small as awakened halflings are, most people mistake them for undead children which is most abhorrent to them. As a result, as cunning and charming as a halfling undead can be, people will often try to destroy these awakened, or else get them to leave town as quickly as possible. As much as the awakened may try to plead their case, most communities will mistake them for a child, making any understanding difficult to come by.

Ability Score Modifier. Your Wisdom score increases by +1.

Size. Awakened Skeleton Halflings average about 3 feet tall and weigh about 40 pounds. Your size is Small.

Speed. Your base walking speed is 25 feet.

Lucky. When you roll a 1 on the d20 for an attack roll, ability check, or saving throw, you can reroll the die and must use the new roll.

Halfling Nimbleness. You can move through the space of any creature that is of a size larger than yours.

Human

Indistinguishable from one Awakened Skeleton to the next, these are the most common type of awakened encountered by travellers. While able to talk and interact with people of all kinds, these undead are still the cause of much fear. This makes many people afraid to deal with even those that seem charming enough. Most awakened undead humans will quickly find themselves in servitude to some undead master, but this is not always the case.

Ability Score Increase. You can increase any two ability scores by +1, except Dexterity. These must be two separate abilities. You cannot add +2 to the same ability score.

Skill Proficiency. You gain proficiency in any two skills of your choice.

Feat. If the gamemaster allows the use of feats, an awakened human may choose a feat at 1st level instead of increasing two ability scores of their choice.

Tiefling

Mostly walking around in hoods and robes, these Awakened Skeletons try to hide their devilish parentage from the communities around them. It is already bad enough that they are undead, but to see that they are undead, and devils is enough to push most innocent people over the edge. There are enough problems with orcs and actual devils running around outside of communities without having to worry about an undead-devil wanting inside your town.

Ability Score Increase. Your Charisma score increases by +1.

Hellish Resistance. You have resistance to fire damage.

Infernal Legacy. You know the thaumaturgy cantrip. When you reach 3rd level, you can cast the hellish rebuke spell as a 2nd level spell once with this trait and regain the ability to do so when you finish a long rest. When you reach 5th level, you can cast the darkness spell once with this trait and regain the ability to do so when you finish a long rest. Charisma is your spellcasting ability for these spells.

Chapter II - Class Options

Being an Awakened Skeleton is a unique choice and often some of the class options in the core rulebook may seem to be conflicting with a character of this type. Below are options that may help in making some classic class options more appropriate for a character of such calibre (or lack of!).

Be sure to consult with your gamemaster before selecting any of the following class options.

Bard College

College of the Grave

Bards of the College of the Grave spend lots of time in musty old libraries and taverns all to learn dark secrets of necromancers long past. While they may not have the magical aptitude of a wizard of the necromancy school, they do have great power over the dead. There is the ability to empower the dead in such a way that makes the undead more dangerous to fight on the battlefield.

These bards travel the world going to the darkest, most depressing towns looking for the dead to raise and empower for their dark desires. Many people do not take to the ominous cloud these bards put out, but the right crowds have been known to find the bard songs of this college quite good. There is a mystical tranquility that makes many of their listeners okay with the idea of dying. While many do not make a habit of trying to die, the crowds find the uncertainty of death quieting, soothing, rather than terrifying.

Bonus Proficiencies

When you join the College of the Grave at 3rd level, you gain proficiency with shields, flails, morningstars and scimitars. You also gain proficiency in two tools of your choice.

Undead Inspiration

Also at 3rd level you can use your Bardic Inspiration to do one of two things: a) you can give advantage to all undead creatures that make an attack, saving throw or skill check within 30 feet of you or b) you can cause all undead creatures to have disadvantage to all attack rolls, saving throws or skill checks within 30 feet. This lasts for a number of rounds equal to your Charisma modifier (minimum of 1).

Extra Spells

Starting at 6th level, you can cast Animate Dead as a regular Bard spell. Instead of adding it to your known spells, you can cast it a number of times per day as your Charisma modifier (minimum of 1).

Spent uses of this feature return after a long rest.

Undead Empowerment

At 14th level you have the power to make the undead stronger and faster, or to slow them down. When you expend one use of Bardic Inspiration you can do one of two things to all undead creatures within 60 feet: a) you can cause them all to increase their walking speed by 10 feet, give them advantage to attacks and give them an extra attack action, or b) you can cause all undead to halve their walking speed, give them disadvantage to all attacks and reduce them to one attack, move or reaction per turn.

Druid Circle

Circle of the Crypt

This circle is seen as the exact opposite that all druids stand for. Most druids avoid those that follow this circle at all costs, while others have found great value in the teachings of these druids. Some of these druids do hold to nefarious ends and seek to put a slavers' hold on the living, but others seek to use the power of death to allow something like life to thrive.

As most other circles fail to observe, the circle of the crypt believes that death is a part of the natural order of life. They know that all things will eventually die and that to understand how to approach the oncoming eventuality of death is a great thing, not something to be feared.

Undead Wild Shape

When you take this circle at 2nd level, you gain the ability to wild shape into an undead creature instead of a normal living animal. You cannot wild shape into a living animal with this circle. The undead creature that you wild shape into follows all the regular rules for wild shape except that your wild shape Dexterity ability has a +2 bonus and you have a +2 bonus to your AC while wild shaped.

Undead Wild Shape Bonus

Upon picking this circle and receiving the wild shape bonus above, you also during the time you are in the form of an undead creature are immune to poison, poison effects and necrotic damage.

As well when you reach 6th level, you can wild shape into any undead animal that has a CR equal to your druid level divided by 4, rounded down.

Necrotic Strike

When you reach 6th level, all your wild shape attacks do an additional d6 necrotic damage. The bonus to your Dexterity while wild shaped increases to +4 and your AC bonus increases to +4.

Celestial Resistance

When you reach 10th level you gain resistance to magic and radiant damage. As well you become immune to necrotic damage.

Grim Visage

At 14th level, you take on a look of death, almost being mistaken for a dead creature yourself. You instill fear on the living and anyone that is not able to pass a Wisdom saving throw of 10 + half your druid level (round down), suffers from the fear condition towards you and your allies.

Fighter Archetype

Death

These warriors have studied and trained in the martial and mystical arts of death for most of their lives. Having been either raised as undead, or simply raised in the worship of a god whose power lies in death and the undead. These haunted fighters go into the world to either fight back the powers of the dead or to bring down the powers of the celestial realm. Most of these fighters have been so indoctrinated in the ways of death that they are unable to think logically or in a good-aligned matter. Some however have started a path to redemption to fight for what is right, as much as their training pushes them the opposite direction.

Necrotic Damage

When you choose this archetype at 3rd level, your weapons damage inflicts necrotic damage on top of the type of damage that your weapon normally does. The necrotic damage does not add to the dice rolled but adds the necrotic energy type to the damage.

Deathly Endurance

Starting at 7th level, the power of death starts to fill up your person. You no longer need to sleep. Instead you enter a meditative state for 4 hours during a long rest. During this time, you are still able to see, hear and respond to those around you, but if you respond to a situation, you will need to start the meditation over again to get the effects of a long rest.

Improved Necrotic Damage

When you reach 10th level, your ability to inflict necrotic damage increases and you now do d8 extra necrotic damage to every target you hit with your weapon.

Healed by Necrosis

Starting at 15th level, you are now healed by necrotic damage. Any damage that is done to you with the necrotic energy type heals you of the amount of damage done. If other energy types are included with the attack, they do normal damage, and the necrotic damage heals you. If you are already healed by necrotic damage, then this effect doubles the amount of hit points healed.

A Roman Awakened Skeleton

Torpor

At 18th level, you effectively become unkillable. If you are reduced to 0 hit points, instead of rolling for death saving throws, you enter a state of torpor and need a month worth of time to regenerate. You can be healed as normal during this time to decrease the time you need to regenerate. The only way to permanently kill you is to banish you to a plane where the dead spend their afterlife.

Paladin Sacred Oath

Oath of Silent Passing

While this oath may seem devoted to the ideals of undeath, the opposite is true. Yes, this oath uses necrotic energy in some of its abilities, but its mission is to ease the dying from life to their eternal destiny. Most of these paladins are far from evil, yet many people will keep a good distance away from them for what they stand for. Death is always a scary subject for many people in any world. These paladins try to ease people into the idea of dying. The time will come when all will cry for the mercies that these paladins offer. Although many try to keep their distance from these oath takers, in the end, they are the ones they want by their bedside as they cross the gates into the life hereafter.

Tenets of Silent Passing

Although the exact tenets and acts of mercy that these paladins offer differ from god to god, they try to maintain a steady doctrine that will help all to understand that they are there for mercy and not judgment.

Forgiveness. Offer forgiveness to those who are weighed down by the wrongs they have done in their life.

Offer Hope. Even to those who may believe they do not qualify for mercy, offer them the hope that they can be redeemed for what they have done.

Sanctification. Help those who ask for forgiveness to understand that they stand holy and pure before the gods themselves. There is no condemnation.

Honour. Only offer the dying the peace they request. Do not take life for the sake of taking life. Let the natural order take care of itself.

End Suffering. If the dying request mercy, offer it to them. Do not allow them to suffer, give them the peace they request.

Oath Spells

You gain oath spells at the paladin levels listed.

Table: Oath of Silent Passing Spells

Paladin Level	Spells
3rd	*sacred flame, spare the dying*
5th	*death ward, guardian of faith*
9th	*mass cure wounds, raise dead*
13th	*create undead, resurrection*
17th	*mass heal, true resurrection*

Necrotic Smite

When you take this oath at 3rd level, your smite damage becomes necrotic energy rather than radiant energy. The damage increases by 1d8 if the target creature is a celestial.

Channel Divinity

When you swear this oath at 3rd level, you gain the following two Channel Divinity options.

Necrotic Energy. As an action, you can imbue one weapon you are holding with necrotic energy using your Channel Divinity. For 1 minute, all damage you deal against a target deals necrotic damage as well as its normal damage. The extra necrotic damage is equal to your Charisma modifier (minimum +1).

You can end this effect on your turn as part of any other action. If you are no longer holding or carrying this weapon, or if you fall unconscious, this effect ends.

Turn the Holy. As an action, you present your gods symbol and speak a damning word that would be offensive to celestial creatures, using your Channel Divinity. Each celestial creature that can see or hear you within 30 feet must make a Wisdom saving throw equal to 10 + your Charisma modifier + your proficiency bonus. If the creature fails its saving throw, it is turned for 1 minute or until it takes damage.

A turned creature spends its turns trying to get as far away from you as it can, and it cannot willingly move to a space within 30 feet of you. It also cannot take reactions. For its action, it can use only the Dash action or try to escape from an effect that prevents it from moving. If there is nowhere to move, the creature can use the Dodge action.

Your Channel Divinity options refresh themselves after a short or long rest.

Necrotic Immunity

Starting at 7th level, you and friendly creatures within 10 feet of you are immune to necrotic energy.

At 18th level, the range of this aura increases to 30 feet.

Shield of the Soul

Starting at 15th level, you are always under the effects of a *shield of faith* spell.

Unholy Nimbus

At 20th level, as an action, you can emanate an aura of darkness. For 1 minute, dark light shines from you in a 30 foot radius. Whenever an enemy creature starts its turn in the darkness, the creature takes 3d6 necrotic damage.

In addition, for the duration, you have advantage on saving throws against spells cast by celestial creatures.

Once you use this feature, you cannot use it again until you finish a long rest.

Warlock Pact

The Dead One

At some point you were visited by a god of death from the pantheon of whatever world you are part of. Rather than refuse him, in the smell and utter decay that filled your vision, you accepted his offer of being your patron. This has had some differing results. At times, you feel guilty for the fascination with death that came with such a patronage, at other times you revel in the power that such a deal came with. Some people in your community became scared of what you represent and continuously petition the local mayor to have you cast out into the wilderness, but for some reason he has yet to do so. If he is given a good enough reason, you have no doubt it would happen. The clerics and paladins of the good part of the pantheon are always looking over their shoulders watching you and waiting for you to make a critical mistake that they can use to make you see once and for all what death really is.

Expanded Spell List

The Dead One lets you choose from an expanded list of spells when you learn a warlock spell. The following spells are added to the warlock spell list for you.

Table: Dead One Expanded Spells

Spell Level	Spells
1st	*inflict wounds, spare the dying*
2nd	*blindness/deafness, protection from poison*
3rd	*animate dead, speak with dead*
4th	*blight, death ward*
5th	*contagion, raise dead*

Feel Life

Beginning at 1st level, your patron gives you the ability to feel life around you. If you spend 1 minute meditating, you can spend the next 10 minutes being able to feel all the living, and undead creatures that are with 60 feet of you. You cannot tell what type of creatures they are, nor how many there are, or anything specific about them. You can just feel that there are living and/or dead things nearby.

Once you use this feature, you cannot use it again until you finish a short or long rest.

Mental Defences

At 6th level you can spend a reaction to become immune to fear and charm effects for 5 minutes. Your patron has shown you so much worse and these things that are trying to frighten or charm you hold nothing over the things you have seen in your dreams.

Once you use this feature, you cannot use it again until you finish a short or long rest.

Dead Bolt

Starting at 10th level, your patron gives you a gift of sending a ball of necrotic energy at your enemies. When you use this ability, you spend an action calling on the bolt and directing it at an enemy creature within 60 feet. If this target fails a Dexterity saving throw equal to 10 + your Charisma modifier + your proficiency bonus it takes 4d6 necrotic damage. This damage is increased to 6d6 at 14th level.

You can use this feature a number of times per day equal to your Charisma modifier (minimum 1). These uses refresh after a long rest.

Aura of the Dead

Starting at 14th level you emit the essence of death all around you. Any enemy creature that is within 60 feet of you must pass a Wisdom saving throw equal to 10 + your Charisma modifier + your proficiency bonus or else take 4d6 damage. This includes all enemy creatures that start their turn within 60 feet of you. Any enemy creature that takes damage from this feature also suffers from the fear condition and must make every effort to get away from you in their next turn.

This feature lasts for a number of rounds equal to your Charisma modifier (minimum 1). All expended uses of this feature refresh after a long rest.

Chapter III - Grave Locations

Everyone needs locations to adventure in and to generally get into trouble around. These locations are perfect places for those adventurers who play on the darker side of things. While more suited for enemy NPC locations or else as a place that you might encounter some powerful foe or secret, keep in mind that these places are steeped in grave magics, where necromantic power infuses everything.

Walk careful brave warrior, or you may become one of the dead ones that you are seeking to fight!

The Temple of Orcus

This is a difficult place to find. Rumours float around that the temple moves around, shifting from place to place using the power of the planes. Those that do find it talk of horrors too terrible to want to remember.

One common feature is that those who do manage to find the temple always recall that it is in a valley of bone. Whether reminiscent of an ancient battle or an intentional mass grave is not certain, but the fact that many innocent people died to create the place where the temple resides is undisputable. The valley is always closed in by dark clouds, the sky looks like its about to storm, often with flashes of blue lightning dancing in the clouds. But it never rains. The dryness and stink of death is everywhere. A rainfall would probably take it all away, but instead it is hot and dry, where no living thing would ever think about taking up residence.

One thing that always stands out is a dark winding, sandy path that leads into the valley and a large shrine deep in the plane of bone. Even though the path winds, adventurers will be able to see the shrine from a distance as they make their way through the place. Ancient, petrified trees sometimes appear that no longer have any semblance of life, blasted into petrification by dark magics that no one wants to recall. Every now and then you will be able to hear a vulture cawing throughout the valley, but the chance of seeing any kind of living bird is very unlikely.

Inhabitants of the Valley

No living thing could ever hope to survive here for long. There simply is no arable land to make that possible. The dirt itself is sandy and lifeless, no green thing grows anywhere that could give anyone hope of making the land farmable in any kind of way. If that is not bad enough, the number of crawling undead that roam around would make things even more difficult.

Skeletons and zombies make up most of the wandering undead that will cause brave or foolish adventurers to walk through here. They care nothing for food or treasure. They just roam, killing every living thing that they come across.

No remorse, no thought about what it is they are doing, just death, everywhere they go. The occasional pack of wights and shadows will also be found here. These are more common the deeper into the valley that the adventurers go. Again, they care for nothing, the wights will more than likely feed on any living flesh, but the shadows will kill without mercy. These creatures can be offered nothing. They have all they need from the dark power of the temple in the heart of the valley. Even though some of these creatures are sentient, and characters might be able to converse with them, they have no needs and nothing an adventurer can offer them will cause them to look away.

The deeper the adventurers go into this place, the more perilous the enemies become. After the wights and shadows have made their attacks, devourers will eventually find the living. These will attack with brutal intensity. The devourers will seek to add a person's undead being to their own miserable existence and will want to imprison their soul for all eternity within themselves. The creatures are relentless, unwavering in their devotion to their dark demon god. Someone can try and fight their way through, but there is a greater chance they may end up serving these creatures in a new unwanted afterlife.

Lastly, as the adventurers finally start to approach the shrine, there are vampires and immediately guarding the temple is a zombie dragon. The vampires will mock and scorn them for their foolishness in coming here. Of course, they will try to drink the characters blood and if they are lucky, turn them into a vampire. Again, they do not really need to drink anyone's blood here. The temple is giving them all the magical subsistence that they require. However, it is in their nature, so regardless of whether they need to feed off someone, they will try. The zombie dragon is mindless and serves no one, but the vampires and Orcus himself. It answers to no one else. It is a devout guardian that will suffer none but the dead to pass. Although it will not enter the temple directly. For whatever reason it simply will not or cannot do so. If adventurers are cunning enough, they may be able to find a way past the undead monstrosity instead of destroying it outright.

Inside the Temple

The dark, gothic architecture of the temple is unmistakable. The brooding air of anger and suffering that this place puts out is palpable. Those that are unprepared for it will find it unnerving, possibly even frightening. If the characters have no resistance or immunity to fear, they will need to pass a Wisdom saving throw of 17 in order not to have the Fear condition added as they explore the temple.

Inside the temple, there is barely any light and the air is cold and dry. Random shivers will crawl down anyone's spine as they make their way through here, whether they have passed the saving throw or not. Effigies of death demons and gods line all the walls, large carved skeletons or images of demon lords that have reigned throughout the ages are engraved on all surfaces most of them in a pose showing subservience.

The most noticeable part of all this grim artwork is the large 100 foot tall statue of Orcus that stands in the middle of the temple. The statue stands tall and proud with a partially shattered dome glass ceiling far above it where the flashes

The statue of Orcus

of lightning can be seen, giving some light to the surroundings. Those without Darkvision will have a difficult time seeing in here. A Wisdom (Perception) check of 13 will make it possible to see normally in here among the shadows and flashes of blue lightning. If a character has Darkvision, they will not need to take the test.

Anyone who dares to approach the statue is in for a very unfortunate surprise. Demons will instantly teleport beside the image as the adventurers get within 30 feet of the effigy. Demons of all kinds of CR's guard the monument, make the CR appropriate for the PC's current level. If the characters continue to be within 30 feet of the likeness of Orcus, the demons will keep attacking. They serve their demon lord without failing and frankly, fear him more than then characters. They will attack in waves. Enemies will not just keep pouring out continuously on the adventurers but instead will wait until one group is destroyed before dispatching the next band of fiends to try and kill the interlopers.

Something Shiny

While the characters are busy fighting for their lives from the demon attacks, have one PC, whoever is closest to the statue, take a Wisdom (Perception) check of a DC 15. If they pass the check, they notice d3 shiny objects at the base of the statue. That character can either make a dash for the objects themself or direct someone from the group to go and check it out.

Upon closer inspection, the character will find 1-3 magic items just laying at the base of the statue. Where they came from is anyone's guess. The most likely source being some brave heroes that never made it out of the place alive, but that died here and are probably wandering around outside in a new state of undeath. The demons will try to pry anyone away from the items as they know these are grand items that can be used to great effect. Check out the chart below to see what kinds of items are found based on the number rolled for.

Table: Types of Magic Items Found

Number of Items	*Types of Items*
1	a rare magic item
2	a rare and very rare magic item
3	a rare, very rare and legendary magic item

Once the magic items are retrieved, the demon attacks will intensify for the remainder of the time that the group is in the temple. Once the adventurers are outside of the temple gates, the demons will halt their pursuit and let the characters go.

Other Features of the Temple

Of course, it is not enough that the characters have all these monsters to deal with in their misguided adventure, there are also environmental issues to deal with.

For one, the air is poisoned, anyone that has to breath or that is not immune to poison and the poisoned condition will have to take a DC 10 Constitution saving throw to avoid becoming poisoned and losing d3 hit points every minute.

This poison is not serious, but it is inconvenient enough that if players are not mindful of the situation, they will quickly find themselves in trouble.

To add to the problems, anyone that is not undead, resistant or immune to necrotic damage, or not serving a god who has suggested domain of Death, must make a DC 17 Wisdom save or take d8 necrotic damage every minute that they are within the temple. This condition is a little more serious and can seriously harm any of the characters who are not mindful of their hit points and how they are being drained, not just by the environment but also by the attacks of the demons.

Anyone who makes the saving throws will not have to worry about these conditions for the remainder of the time they are within the temple. If they leave and come back, the test will have to be retaken. Anyone that failed the test, can of course, leave and come back in and then retake the saving throw and maybe this time, they will pass it.

Lastly, once the magic items are taken, or stolen, the necrotic damage increases to 2d6 damage every minute. So once the items are taken, it is critical that the characters get out of there as quickly as possible!

Getting Out Alive

Once the party has managed to get out of the temple, they should not have that much difficulty getting out of the valley. Some undead may impede their heroic escape, but for the most part, the roaming dead will be too preoccupied with what happened at the temple and the angry sounds of Orcus coming from some ethereal reality, to care about the characters trying to escape with their prize. If the gamemaster wants, he can have the PC's hear some voice just as they are about to get out of the crest of the valley swear vengeance on them. This voice is deep and terrible and can only come from Orcus himself.

The Mael-Carin Crypt

This family crypt has been part of the Mael-Carin legacy for centuries. The family is a mostly good standing family who are shrewd businesspeople and always out to make money. While most would suspect them of mistreatment of workers and slavery, they are fair and honourable employers who treat their workers with more equity than most other merchants around.

There is however, one dark secret. An ancestor of theirs from back when the business was first founded, was into dark magic and played around with the necromantic arts on a frequent basis. Many in the family have attempted to bury this secret since accusations of where the wealth has come from have bounced around for longer than most people can remember. Some people accept the turn the family seems to have made. Others however hold this over their heads.

As part of that dark secret, the family often hires adventurers to enter the family crypt and clean out the undead that always seem to show up there. They are not certain what is drawing them to the location, but they have heard rumours of a vampire residing deep within the tomb. Some have claimed that the vampire is really the long dead relative that played with undead magics, but this is unconfirmed. If the family knows the identity of the undead lord in their crypt, they have made no mention of it. Chances are highly likely that they do.

The Cemetery and Surrounding Area

The cemetery that the crypt is in was at one time a burial place for the rich. Many finely ornate tombs and graves can be found here. Beautiful sculptures of the deceased as well as carvings of angels and other celestial creatures are all over the large plot of land.

Over the years, with the problems in the Mael-Carin crypt, the cemetery has seen a sharp decline in the people interred here. The place has become a byword of a curse used to scare children. Many times, parents will frighten children with stories of the creatures buried here, then tell them if they do not go to sleep, they will be buried in one of the mass graves that now inhabit the cemetery.

This is not untrue. Since the money has been taken out of the cemetery from the community, the place has fallen into disrepair and is used to bury mass pits of the dead who cannot afford to be properly buried. Many stone markers indicate where large pits have been dug up to inter many of the poor, homeless, or unknown wanderers that die in the town. Even adventurers that have tried to clean out the crypt have been buried in these mass graves.

Few workers visit the cemetery in recent years. The place holds a dark foreboding, and many have spoken of ghostly whispers that emanate from the various graves, especially the crypt. Those that are brave enough to come into the property to maintain it will go nowhere near the family crypt. Horror stories have been passed around among the workers of the strange things that happen around that building, often resulting in mysterious disappearances that no one can explain.

The mass graves here are unfortunately part of the problem. Whatever creature that has called the Mael-Carin crypt its home uses the mass graves to create more of its undead servants. The city suspects this, but they can find no other place that will allow these graves to be dug.

Coming into the Cemetery

Anyone going into the plot of land will immediately feel a cold chill run down their spines. Whether this is just from the air of the cemetery or the feeling of magic will be unknown to those without magic training. Those who can use magic will be able to sense naturally that this cold chill is from the arcane. Those that are able make an Intelligence (Arcana) DC 10 check will be able to tell that the cold chill comes from necrotic energy. This should be enough to tell the adventurers that there is something evil here. It is not just stories and urban legends, but actual necromantic power that infuses this entire place.

Wandering around the graves and few other crypts that inhabit the place will not turn up anything significant. The adventurers may at times see a wisp of mist that looks like a ghost or wraith, but there will be nothing for sure. A chance that a real wraith will show up is possible, but only if the gamemaster rolls a 18-20 on a d20 for every hour the PC's spend in the cemetery.

The Mael-Carin Crypt

The Mael-Carin crypt itself is not difficult to find. It is the biggest and most ornate building in the cemetery. Even though the building has fallen into some disrepair, it is evident that whoever originally built the place did so with a lot of care. Any dwarf in the party will immediately be impressed with the quality of the stonework. In fact, any dwarf will probably swear by their beard that only a dwarf could have built something of such beauty. They would not be wrong.

Into the Dark

The crypt door is already broken down so there is no problem entering and descending the stairs. The smell however is of dankness, and decaying and rotting flesh. Anyone that fails a DC 10 Constitution save will automatically start to feel sick just walking in here. Cobwebs are strewn across the passageways and when adventurers enter the first room, there is dust, scurrying rats and some piles of bones scattered all over the floor. It is entirely up to the gamemaster of how many rooms or which direction all the rooms lead but remember that the crypt is quite large and goes deeply into the earth.

For each room that the adventurers enter, the gamemaster should roll a d20 and consult the chart below.

Table: Encounter Results

d20 Result	*Encounter*
1-10	nothing
11-15	1d4 zombies, 1d3 skeletons
16-18	1d8 zombies, 1d4 skeletons
19-20	1d6 zombies, 1 wight

Each room will also have d3 sarcophagi that the PC's are able to search. Of course, if the family ever hears that the party is looting their crypt, the characters may have more problems in the future as the family seeks to get those items back!

Hidden Treasure

For each of the sarcophagi that the adventurers search, roll on the table below.

Table: Loot

d20 Result	*Loot*
1-14	nothing but bones
15-17	d10 sp, d6 gp
18-19	d10 gp, 1 common magic item
20	2d6 gp, 1 uncommon magic item

Remember that the Mael-Carin family will want these magic items returned to them if the characters manage to get them out of the crypt. The overall street value of common and uncommon items is not that grand, but they will cause the family to exact revenge and want payment for any items that they have traded, sold or lost that were not returned to them.

The Vampire

Evidently, what lies in the deepest parts of the family crypt is a vampire. Gamemasters are free to create whatever story they feel is appropriate to add to the lore of why the vampire is there. The creature could in fact be the ancestor of the family, or it could just be some other vampire's spawn that has taken up residence here. Try not to make the vampire a difficult encounter, lower the CR on the bestiary monster a few levels to make it easier for lower level characters, or higher for those with more experience.

The most notable thing about the vampire is a gold mask it is wearing. What the family will not tell the group is the vampire has been destroyed before yet keeps coming back. The reason is the mask. When the vampire dies while wearing it, the creature returns to life the next night. Even if the mask is removed after it is dead, the creature will still return. The trick is to get the mask off the vampire while it is still "alive" and then kill it. Or else, to return the next night and destroy the creature when it is not wearing the mask. The vampire will always know where the mask is when it comes back to life, as the last person to wear the mask will always know its location.

Mael-Carin Death Mask

Wonderous Item, rare (requires attunement)

If an undead creature dies while wearing this mask, it will rise with full hit points the next night. As well, the creature will always know where the mask is until another creature puts it on.

If a living creature puts on the mask, they can cast Create Undead, with advantage to any rolls they might make, as well, they are immune to necrotic damage.

OPEN GAME LICENSE Version 1.0a

The following text is the property of Wizards of the Coast, Inc. and is Copyright 2000 Wizards of the Coast, Inc ("Wizards"). All Rights Reserved.

1. Definitions: (a)"Contributors" means the copyright and/or trademark owners who have contributed Open Game Content; (b)"Derivative Material" means copyrighted material including derivative works and translations (including into other computer languages), potation, modification, correction, addition, extension, upgrade, improvement, compilation, abridgment or other form in which an existing work may be recast, transformed or adapted; (c) "Distribute" means to reproduce, license, rent, lease, sell, broadcast, publicly display, transmit or otherwise distribute; (d)"Open Game Content" means the game mechanic and includes the methods, procedures, processes and routines to the extent such content does not embody the Product Identity and is an enhancement over the prior art and any additional content clearly identified as Open Game Content by the Contributor, and means any work covered by this License, including translations and derivative works under copyright law, but specifically excludes Product Identity. (e) "Product Identity" means product and product line names, logos and identifying marks including trade dress; artifacts; creatures characters; stories, storylines, plots, thematic elements, dialogue, incidents, language, artwork, symbols, designs, depictions, likenesses, formats, poses, concepts, themes and graphic, photographic and other visual or audio representations; names and descriptions of characters, spells, enchantments, personalities, teams, personas, likenesses and special abilities; places, locations, environments, creatures, equipment, magical or supernatural abilities or effects, logos, symbols, or graphic designs; and any other trademark or registered trademark clearly identified as Product identity by the owner of the Product Identity, and which specifically excludes the Open Game Content; (f) "Trademark" means the logos, names, mark, sign, motto, designs that are used by a Contributor to identify itself or its products or the associated products contributed to the Open Game License by the Contributor (g) "Use", "Used" or "Using" means to use, Distribute, copy, edit, format, modify, translate and otherwise create Derivative Material of Open Game Content. (h) "You" or "Your" means the licensee in terms of this agreement.

The License: This License applies to any Open Game Content that contains a notice indicating that the Open Game Content may only be Used under and in terms of this License. You must affix such a notice to any Open Game Content that you Use. No terms may be added to or subtracted from this License except as described by the License itself. No other terms or conditions may be applied to any Open Game Content distributed using this License.

Offer and Acceptance: By Using the Open Game Content You indicate Your acceptance of the terms of this License.

Grant and Consideration: In consideration for agreeing to use this License, the Contributors grant You a perpetual, worldwide, royalty-free, non- exclusive license with the exact terms of this License to Use, the Open Game Content.

Representation of Authority to Contribute: If You are contributing original material as Open Game Content, You represent that Your Contributions are Your original creation and/or You have sufficient rights to grant the rights conveyed by this License.

Notice of License Copyright: You must update the COPYRIGHT NOTICE portion of this License to include the exact text of the COPYRIGHT NOTICE of any Open Game Content You are copying, modifying or distributing, and You must add the title, the copyright date, and the copyright holder's name to the COPYRIGHT NOTICE of any original Open Game Content you Distribute.

Use of Product Identity: You agree not to Use any Product Identity, including as an indication as to compatibility, except as expressly licensed in another, independent Agreement with the owner of each element of that Product Identity. You agree not to indicate compatibility or co-adaptability with any Trademark or Registered Trademark in conjunction with a work containing Open Game Content except as expressly licensed in another, independent Agreement with the owner of such Trademark or Registered Trademark. The use of any Product Identity in Open Game Content does

www.ingramcontent.com/pod-product-compliance
Lightning Source LLC
LaVergne TN
LVHW010549100826
845148LV00013B/2672

* 9 7 8 1 7 7 3 5 6 4 1 1 1 *